THE DIRTY GREAT DINOSAUR

For Katie, Sophie and Sam,
and wee baby Theo – M.W.
For my dad, Richard – L.L.

ORCHARD BOOKS
338 Euston Road, London NW1 3BH
Orchard Books Australia
Level 17/207 Kent Street, Sydney, NSW 2000
First published in 2009 by Orchard Books
First published in paperback in 2009

ISBN 978 1 40830 359 7

Text © Martin Waddell 2009
Illustrations © Leonie Lord 2009

The rights of Martin Waddell to be identified as the author
and of Leonie Lord to be identified as the illustrator of this work
have been asserted by them in accordance with the Copyright,
Designs and Patents Act, 1988.

A CIP catalogue record for this book is available from the British Library.

11

Printed in China

Orchard Books is a division of Hachette Children's Books,
an Hachette UK company.
www.hachette.co.uk

THE DIRTY GREAT DINOSAUR

Martin Waddell & Leonie Lord

Grrrrr!

ORCHARD

Tweet!

Purr!

Hal and his little dog, Billy,
were playing in Hal's garden, when . . .

Grrrrrrr!

A Dirty Great Dinosaur
charged in.

Miaow!

"I'm hungry and I've come to eat you!" roared the Dirty Great Dinosaur.

"I am small, and eating small children is not really fair," Hal replied, politely.

"Then I'll eat your mum!" roared the Dirty Great Dinosaur.

"Then I'll eat your dad instead!" roared the Dirty Great Dinosaur.

"No way!
I love my mum,"
Hal exclaimed.

"I love my dad too, and
I'd miss him," Hal told
the Dirty Great
Dinosaur.

"Then I'll eat your
little dog, Billy!" roared the
Dirty Great Dinosaur.

Billy was scared but . . .

"OH NO, YOU WON'T!" shouted Hal.

"Oh yes, I will!"
roared the Dirty Great Dinosaur.

Grrrrrrr!

Grrrrrrrr!

Grrrrrrrrrr!

"Go for it, Billy!"

shouted Hal.

"Got you!" smiled Hal.

"Do you give in?" shouted Hal.

Grrrrrrrr! grrred the Dirty Great Dinosaur.

"Apologise to us and put our garden back right and promise not to eat people or dogs ever again!" Hal told the Dirty Great Dinosaur.

"I'm sorry,"
gulped the
Dirty Great Dinosaur . . .

and it cleaned up the mess it had made.

"Oh dear, I'm still hungry!"
the Dirty Great Dinosaur sighed
in a tiny-little-dinosaur voice.

And so . . .

... Hal's mum made a Dirty Great Dinosaur dinner and the Dirty Great Dinosaur ate it.

"Thank you so much!"
the Dirty Great Dinosaur
said to Hal and
Hal's mum.

"Do call again," said Hal's dad.

And the Dirty Great Dinosaur ran off as fast as
a Dirty Great Dinosaur can go.

"Well done, Hal
and our Billy,"
said Hal's mum.

"That was super, son!"
said Hal's dad, and
he patted Hal's head.

And that's how Hal and Billy saved everyone
from the Dirty Great Dinosaur.